Dedicated to

the memory

of the late,

great defender

of predators,

Dick Randall.

EVERYBODY'S SOMEBODY'S LUNCH

Cherie Mason

Illustrated by Gustav Moore

TILBURY HOUSE • PUBLISHERS • GARDINER, MAINE

"Mooouuuuser! Where are you!"

Her cat had been gone overnight, so in the morning she started looking for him in the woods that surrounded her family's saltwater farm.

She loved walking in the shadows of the spruce and fir. In
the spring she would search for wild lady slippers. She knew where
they grew in pink profusion, but she kept it a secret to protect
them. As the days warmed, the ferns and bracken opened like giant

ladies' fans, feathering the forest floor with such lushness that she

didn't dare put a foot down among them. Little meadow voles

and red squirrels went about their business not even noticing her —

maybe because she was there so much and she moved so quietly.

Often she would take along a basket still stained from last summer's blueberries and, depending on the season, fill it with delectable ostrich-fern fiddleheads in May, tiny wild cranberries for Thanksgiving dinner in late summer, and, finally, pine cones and acorns to tuck in the Christmas wreaths she and her mother made each year.

In winter, if the snow wasn't too deep, she loved to follow the straight-line tracks of the red fox, which sometimes followed the big, flat ones of the snowshoe hare. These woods were in her heart, they were her favorite place to be, and today everything felt especially lovely and peaceful.

But as she glanced to the side of the path, what she saw shook her down to her toes. There lay Mouser's red collar, and all around it, bloody bits of fur.

Stunned, the girl reached for a fallen tree trunk and sat down. Holding the collar, she remembered how much fun Mouser had been, especially as a kitten. How he would chase a paper ball on the end of a string, how he would pounce on a rubber mouse. But she didn't take him with her on her walks in the woods because he'd scare away the birds and animals she loved to watch. No harm must come to any of them. She loved every living thing. She could never set a trap for a mouse or step on a spider.

She began to cry. Who could have done this terrible thing? Her father had mentioned that a coyote had been seen nearby. Last night, while she was sleeping and dreaming, had the coyote crept up on Mouser and killed him?

Just then a chickadee hopped to a branch right over her and cocked its head. A leaf rustled near her foot, and out popped a shrew no bigger than her thumb. It saw her and stood up on its hind legs, putting up its tiny paws in a threatening gesture, like a prizefighter. Then the little creature turned, pushed its nose into the leaf litter, pulled out a fat earthworm, and proceeded to eat it like a string of spaghetti.

She knew about shrews. Her grandmother had told her about them. The old woman was fascinated by shrews.

"From that little bundle of fur you can learn astonishing things," Granny had said. She told her that short-tailed shrews ate their weight in food every day. Just missing one meal could be the end of them. They even have a poisonous bite. It all added up, she said, to their being one of the fiercest hunters in the world!

The shrew scurried around frantically, looking for more food. It found a small berry and gobbled it down, then a beetle, then a slug, then a few ants. Suddenly the grass parted and a small, slender snake slid up silently from behind, hoping to take the shrew by surprise. As it slithered forward, the little shrew spun around and, amazing as it seemed, attacked the snake! The shrew dug in with its venomous teeth, the snake struggled a bit and then went limp. As the shrew slowly began to nibble on its prey, the girl had to turn away. She held Mouser's collar to her heart.

Through her tears her eye caught the sparkles on a large cobweb stretched across the branch of a juniper. In the center of the strong spokes of the web crouched a rather large brown spider. At the outer edge of the web a horsefly wrapped in the spider's silk struggled hopelessly. She didn't want to watch, but she did. The eight-legged, eight-eyed spider slid down the thread of the web, sank its fangs into the fly, and began to suck out its life.

That was enough! Today everything seemed to be death and killing. She ran home.

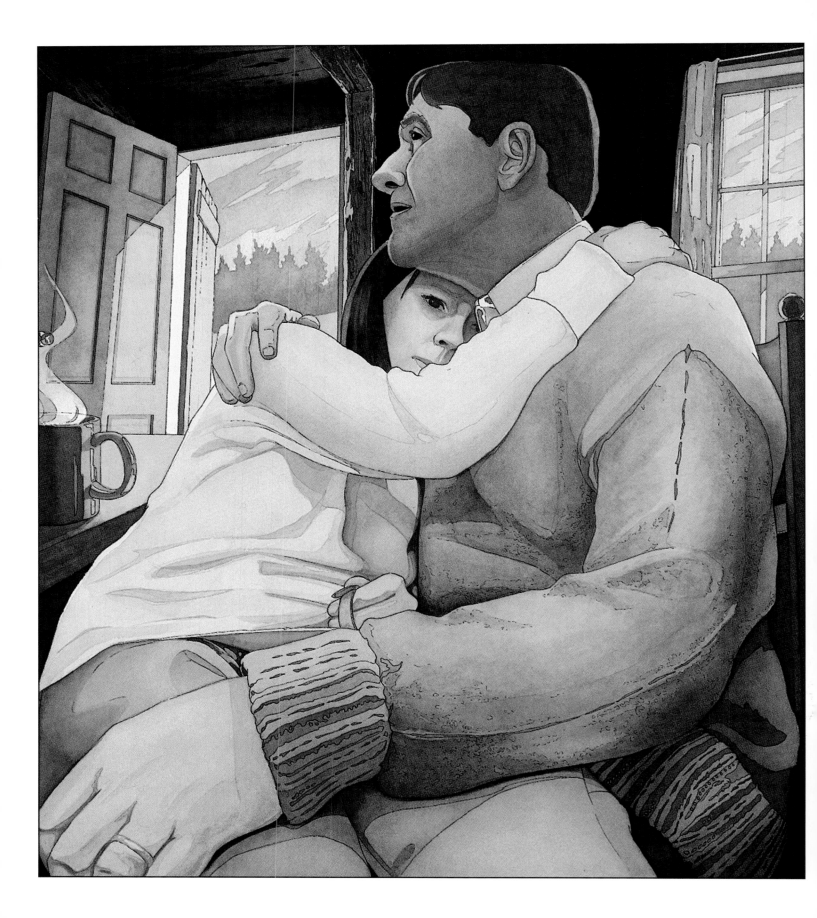

Bursting into the house and into the arms of her startled father, she told him what had happened to Mouser. As he comforted her, she also told him between sobs about the shrew and the snake and the spider. "Did a coyote get Mouser?"

"It's possible," her father explained, "but it could have been some other wild animal. The ways of nature are sometimes difficult to accept. It isn't all roses and butterflies out there. The spider eats the fly, the shrew eats the snake, and maybe next time a snake will eat the shrew — and so it goes. Everybody's somebody's lunch. Everybody has to eat. Even us." He said she should ask at school about "predators": animals that kill other animals to eat and to live. It might help her understand.

The next day was Monday, and on Mondays her teacher would ask the class to tell what they had done during the weekend, something that might be unusual or interesting. When it was her turn, she painfully described finding the remains of Mouser and finally asked if he had been killed by a "predator."

The teacher replied that what had happened to her cat was very sad, but Mouser had ventured into the wild world of predator and prey, where he didn't belong.

She went on to explain that in nature, predators and prey balance each other. Plant-eaters are food for the meat-eaters. And that's good, because there are far more prey animals like mice and rabbits and deer than predatory animals. Without the meat-eaters, the plant-eaters would multiply and multiply. For example, there can be so many deer that they overeat their food supply and then starve. By killing some deer, predators such as coyotes and wolves keep the deer herds smaller so there's more food. And in turn, if there are too few deer to feed the coyotes, the coyotes have fewer pups. In this way, the prey keep the number of predators under control.

Now everyone in class began to raise a hand with something to say.

"I feel sorry for the squirrel when the fox chases it," said one boy. "I hope it gets away."

"But what about the fox?" asked the teacher. "Do we want the fox to starve? Do we care about the fox's pups? They're hungry, too."

"You see, there are no bad or mean animals. After all, Mouser was a predator, too! He killed more mice and birds and snakes than anyone knew about, and he didn't even need to kill to eat. I bet he always had a nice bowl of catfood waiting at home."

When the girl boarded the school bus to go home that afternoon, she sat alone. She had much to think about.

When she arrived at her stop, instead of going into the house, she headed on down the road to Granny's. She needed to talk to her. Inside, settled at the worn wooden kitchen table with a glass of milk and a plate of warm muffins, she looked across at her grandmother and told her about Mouser's terrible death. She had already learned so much from the woman with white hair and a light step who taught her the names of the flowers and the habits of the animals. Granny once announced proudly that there was Passamaquoddy blood in her veins. Native people were closer to nature than others, she said. One day they both had been sitting very quietly for a long, long time (that was the secret to watching wild creatures, Granny said) near an opening in a large granite rock. Finally they were rewarded for their patience. One by one, out tumbled the most adorable fox puppies, yipping eagerly. Their mother appeared at that moment carrying a squirrel in her mouth, and the hungry babies all followed her back into the cave. She would never forget the sight.

Granny agreed with everything the teacher had said about predators and prey, but she had a tale of her own to add. It was this:

An Indian chief and his youngest son were

passing through an open meadow when,

swifter than a heartbeat, a golden eagle raced

down on a small hare feeding near the brook.

In an instant, the screaming, struggling

animal in the strong grip of the eagle's talons

was carried to the clouds, where they both

disappeared. The boy gasped. The father

turned to him and said, "Do not be troubled,

my son. What you have seen is the sacred

way of the earth. The death of the hare is

the gift of life to the eagle."

A few days later, when the weather was fair and the tide high, the girl went to one of her favorite places, a small island that lay close to shore. After just a short row in her peapod, she beached the boat. A blue heron stood in the sea grasses, feeding. She stopped and watched. She knew now that this elegant bird she had always admired was indeed a predator. It ate fish and eels, of course, but even mice and snakes. Who would have imagined it? She picked her way through the rockweed and climbed up a ledge. From there it was into the trees to a hidden clearing covered with bright green mounds of pincushion moss.

She flopped down on the spongy, sweet-smelling carpet and wished herself up, up into the sky where the hawks were being wafted on winds that would carry them south. How gracefully they glided. She had known they attacked and ate other birds, but now she knew that most of their prey got away. Like all predators, they had to try again and again in order to eat. They had babies to feed.

Each spring she watched the osprey return to a nest in the highest tree on the island. Soon the chicks would peek out over the edge of the nest, waiting for mom or dad to return with a nice fish. She remembered how the parents would screech and dive-bomb any crow or other bird that came too close. They doted on

their little brood. Just then a daddy-long-legs marched over her
arm. As she brushed it off she wondered, is it predator or prey?

Even the clouds looked like lions and tigers chasing
elephants. Gradually the softness of her forest bed put her to sleep.
She dreamed wistfully of a wolf and a moose grazing peacefully
beside each other in an endless meadow of grass and wildflowers.

When she woke up, it was almost dark. She rushed back to the beach, only to find her little boat high and dry. The tide was going out.

It took many tugs to haul the boat down to the water. Getting in, she rowed as fast as she could. The light was fading quickly. By the time she reached the opposite shore, it was totally dark. "Oh, no," she said out loud, "there's no moon tonight." Sliding the peapod up onto the rocks, above the reach of the morning tide, she tied the painter to a small tree and headed in the direction she thought would lead home.

Now the ground that was always so familiar in the daylight felt as strange as a different planet. She reached out to touch a tree or a bush, trying to find a path. An owl hooted right overhead. She hadn't heard it coming. But then she remembered that some owls can fly so noiselessly mice can't hear them. Moving forward slowly in the blackness, she picked up the musky scent of a fox.

    Something brushed past her cheek. A bat?! Her heart began to pound. They were out at night hunting flying insects. She knew they wouldn't hurt her, but it made her uneasy. What else was out there in the darkness? Something moved in the dry leaves, a twig snapped. She wouldn't like to scare a skunk! Would a prey animal know what that sound meant?

Just then a single tree frog let loose its cheerful, birdlike chirping. She took it as a good sign, and sure enough, off in the distance, little squares of light appeared through the trees. The girl pushed through the brush and soon was out in the open field of the farm. She had made it! She had found her way home! But there was more to it than that. She understood so much more now. She had grown up in many ways these past few days.

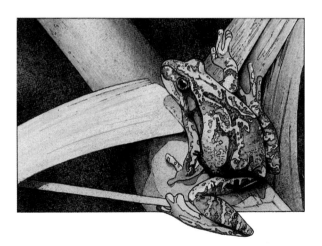

She stopped to make sure the chicken coop gate was locked against foxes and raccoons. As delicious smells of dinner reached her, she thought, "Mother doesn't have to dive in the ocean or set out a web or hunt all day and night to feed the family. Yet we eat birds and eggs and animals. So what kind of predator are we?"

Her wondering and discovering had only begun.

As she opened the kitchen door, she realized that Mouser would never again greet her.

Her mother called, "Is that you, dear girl?"

In a voice that sounded not at all like her old self but older and wiser, she answered, "Yes, it's me, Mother. I'm home."

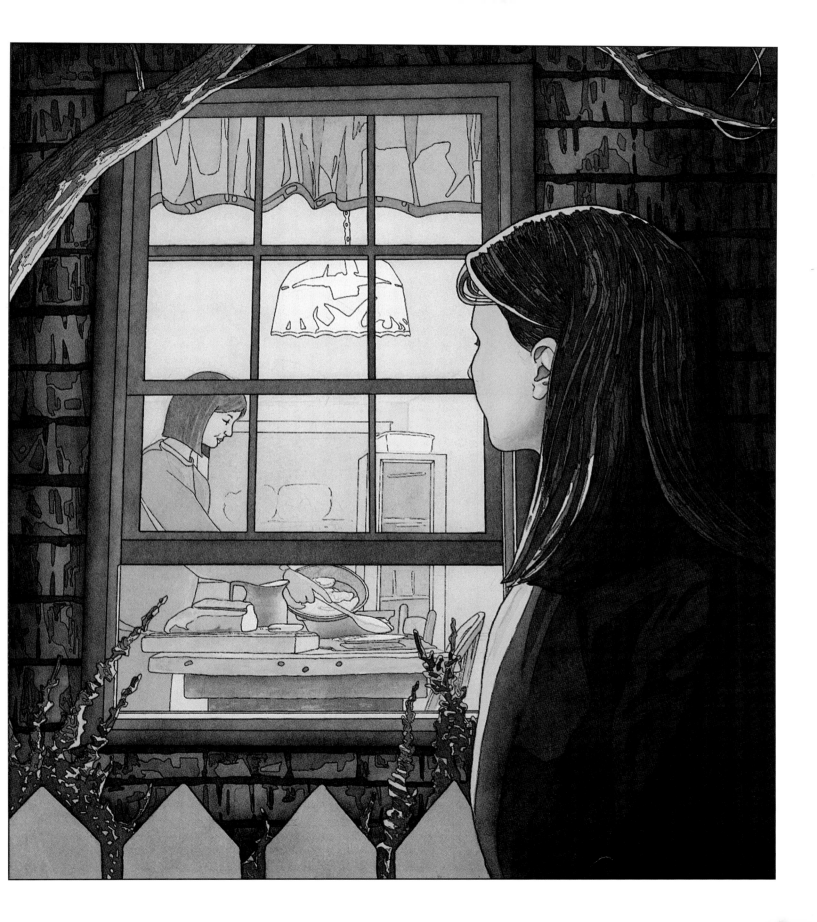

Tilbury House, Publishers
2 Mechanic Street
Gardiner, Maine 04345
800-582-1899 • www.tilburyhouse.com

First printing: October, 1998. First paperback printing: November, 2001.

10 9 8 7 6 5 4 3 2

Illustrations by Gustav Moore, Portland, Maine
Design and Layout: Geraldine Millham, Westport, Massachusetts
Editorial and Production: Jennifer Elliott, Barbara Diamond, Mackenzie Dawson
Color Scans and Film: Integrated Composition Systems, Spokane, Washington
Printing and Binding: Worzalla Publishing, Stevens Point, Wisconsin

Library of Congress Cataloging-in-Publication Data
Mason, Cherie
Everybody's somebody's lunch / Cherie Mason ; illustrations by Gustav Moore.
p.   cm.
Summary: A young girl learns about predators and prey in the animal world when her cat Mouser is killed by a coyote.
ISBN 0-88448-198-0 (hc : alk. paper) ISBN 0-88448-200-6 (pb : alk. paper)
[1. Predatory animals—Fiction. 2. Animals—Fiction. 3. Nature—Fiction] I. Moore, Gustav, ills. II. Title.
PZ7.M3835Ev   1998
[Fic]—dc21   98-38915
                                               CIP
                                               AC

Also Available:
EVERYBODY'S SOMEBODY'S LUNCH TEACHER'S GUIDE
THE ROLE OF PREDATOR AND PREY IN NATURE
Cherie Mason and Judy Kellogg Markowsky
Illustrations by Rosemary Giebfried

Paperback, $9.95   ISBN 0-88448-199-9
8½ x 11, 80 pages, illustrations   Education/Nature; Grades 3–6

This Teacher's Guide provides educators with information, activities, and play that can easily be incorporated into wildlife and nature study programs. Included are the history of the persecution of predators due to human ignorance and fear; profiles of predatory mammals, invertebrates, reptiles, amphibians, birds, and marine life; humans as predators; and hopeful evidence of change in today's attitudes. These critical environmental lessons are structured so that they are interesting, instructive, and fun.

   Judy Markowsky is the director of Maine Audubon's Fields Pond Nature Center, has an Ed.D. in Science Education, and has created award-winning environmental education programs.